T0197374

WILLIAM T. BIX

illUstRatIOns by MaRk RUBEn abacaJan

THEOdORE
In THE
DARK

Print information available on the last page

Rev. date: 04/04/2016

To order additional copies of this book, contact:
Xlibris
1-888-795-4274
www.Xlibris.com
Orders@Xlibris.com

Theodore
in the Dark

William T. Bix

Illustrations by
Mark Ruben Abacajan

Theodore was extremely afraid of the dark. When the lights went out, everything and every shadow appeared to him as the most terrible of monsters.

Theodore's parents explained to him with great patience that these things were not monsters. Theodore understood his parents, but he could not stop feeling an awful fear whenever it was dark.

One day, his grandma Wilhelmina came to visit. Grandma was a wise, sweet, incredible woman. She was famous for her courage and for having gone on many journeys of adventures. Some of which were made into books and movies.

Theodore wanted to conquer his fear of the dark, so he asked his grandma how she became so brave and if she had ever been frightened.

"A great many times, Theodore," answered his grandma. "I remember when I was small and I was terribly afraid of the dark. I couldn't stay in the dark for even a moment."

Theodore became very excited. "How was it possible that someone so courageous could have been afraid of the dark?"

"I will tell you a secret, Theodore. It was a blind friend who taught me to be brave. The secret is to change your eyes. Since blind people can't see, their hands are their eyes. All you have to do to conquer your fear is what they do. Close the eyes on your face, and open the eyes of your hands."

"Let's make a deal. Tonight when you go to bed and put out the lights, if anything makes you afraid, close your eyes, carefully get out of bed, and try to see what it is that is making you scared, but do it using your hands as eyes. Tomorrow tell me how you're getting on with your fear."

Theodore accepted, but he was rather worried. He knew he would need to be brave to close his eyes and go touch whatever it was that was frightening him.

When Theodore's parents took him to bed, he himself put out the light. After a while, he felt afraid of one of the shadows that was in the bedroom. Following the advice of his grandma Wilhelmina, he closed the eyes on his face and opened the eyes of his hands. Theodore was building up his courage, and he went over to touch the mysterious shadow.

The next morning, Theodore came running into the kitchen, a big smile on his face and a song on his lips. The monster is soft and smooth! He shouted, "*It's my teddy bear!*"

Strategies for Overcoming Nighttime Fears

Here are some tips to help your child overcome nighttime fears.

*Do not support belief in your child's imaginative creatures.

*Reinsure your child's safety.

*Work on building your child's self-confidence and coping skills.

*Keep the bedtime routine light, happy, and fun.

*Allow night lights and security objects.

*Don't forget positive reinforcement and/or reward programs.

*Have fun in the dark.

*Avoid scary television shows.

*Have relaxation training.

Allow your child to talk about their fears in the daytime. They may be able to express their fears more clearly during the day, which will help you support those coping skills and build their self-confidence.

Good night, sweet dreams.

Printed in the United States
By Bookmasters